MW00823582

Everything Changed After The Baby

Written By: Jaa'Lisa Banks

Illustrated By: Kenyon Brady

EDUCATIONAL PSYCHOLOGY
PUBLISHING

MYND-BEHAVIOR WELLNESS

Copyright © 2020 by TTE Educational Psychology Publishing and Jaa'Lisa Banks

Illustration Copyright © 2020 by TTE Educational Psychology Publishing and Kenyon Brady

All rights reserved. No part of this book may be used or reproduced in any form or by any electronic or mechanical means, including photocopying, recording, or by any information storage and retrieval system, without written permission in writing from the publisher, except for brief quotations used in articles and reviews.

ISBN: 9780997031386

Editor: Tamara Taylor

Book Cover Designer & Illustrator: Kenyon Brady

TTE Educational Psychology Publishing
www.ttepublishing.com

To my husband, kids, and my friend Tessa for her resiliency and her constant encouragement.

Jaa'Lisa Banks

Before you were born, I couldn't believe that I was going to have a baby. Your daddy looked at me with tears in his eyes, and we hugged each other for what seemed like forever. We were so happy that we cried. Our hearts fluttered with joy when we thought about you being part of our lives. We would dream about what you would look like. Who's eyes you would have, or if you would have your daddy's dimple or mommy's stubby little toes? Would you have kinky or wavy hair? Or would it be straight like your grandma's? It was all so exciting and waiting for you to arrive seemed impossible.

On the day you were born, I couldn't even speak. I didn't know what to say. You were so beautiful, and you were here! You were more than what I expected you to be. I didn't know that I could love someone that I just met so much. Looking at you was more than I could stand as I marveled at each tiny breath you took.

When the nurses took you away to bathe you and run tests to make sure you were healthy, I counted every minute until they brought you back. I didn't sleep all night. I just looked at you. I put my finger up to your nose to make sure you were still breathing. When you would make any kind of noise I checked to make sure everything was okay. I wanted to make sure all your needs were being met at all times.

As you got older, we enjoyed our time together. I got to stay home with you while your daddy went to work. Those were some of the best days. We spent so much time making up imaginary worlds together that only you and I existed in. We played everywhere together, but some of the greatest moments were when we got out and explored the real world.

At the park we would lay on the grass. One time I remembered that I put my hand on your heart and shut my eyes for a moment. As the steady beating inside your chest reminded me of the first time the doctor let me hear your heartbeat, the wind whistled through the trees and sent a chill down my spine. I felt that feeling that you gave me on the day you were born. It was my greatest joy to be your mommy. This was what I was made for.

Each night we would snuggle up close together with your body perfectly nestled into mine. This was the best part of my day as we would read our favorite books and recite lines together, laugh, and sing. I would then put the books away and get you ready for bed. Your eyes would already be low as I would lie you down. I would carefully place your blankets around you, making sure your favorite teddy was right next to you.

10

would breathe you in as I leaned down to give you a kiss. Each night I still felt like
didn't spend enough time with you that day. I always wanted to do more, and to
ave more moments, but I knew we both needed sleep so we could have more fun
e next day.

You were growing up so fast and before I knew it, you were starting school. This meant that we would not spend as much time together, and I had a hard time imagining what my days would be like without you. I felt like my heart was being separated from my body. To even think about spending so much time away from you was almost too much for me to handle. Each day I would wait for your school bus to teeter tot down the street. As I heard the sound of the air being released from the brakes and the big doors creak open, my heart grew bigger and bigger as you ran closer to me.

When I held you in my arms I felt whole again. I never felt okay when you were away at school. Sometimes, I would just stare at you when you told me about your day. I would take mental pictures of you enjoying your snack, and swinging your feet happily at the table. I would often think about how amazing you were when I first held you and looked into your eyes. I have seen many things in my lifetime, but nothing would ever be as incredible as you.

13

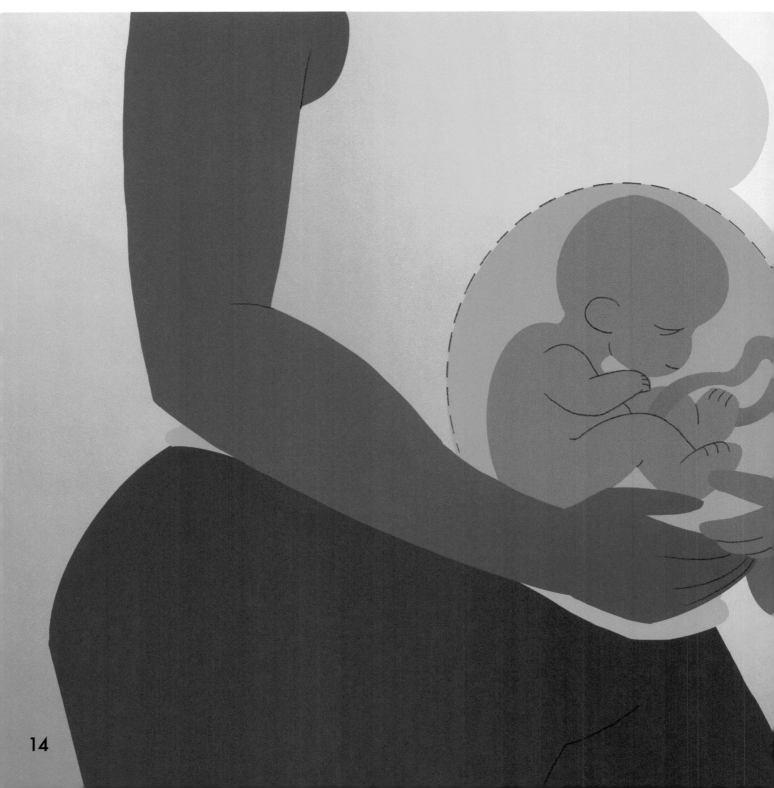

When I thought things couldn't get any better and my heart couldn't possibly get any bigger, we found out we were having another baby. It was going to be a girl! We were thrilled! All of the familiar feelings that I had with you came rushing back to me. I couldn't believe that I was lucky enough to be able to have two of you! You loved talking to my belly and making so many plans for you and your sister.

When I had your sister, my heart grew twice as big. I didn't think it was possible to love anyone as much as I loved you, but I did! It seemed like my life was complete! I couldn't wait to get her home so we could start our new routine with your sister included.

You held her for the first time, and it was the most precious thing that I had ever seen. In those moments I didn't think life could get any better, but quickly things started to change. That feeling of happiness started to fade, and I couldn't understand why. I started to get worried about leaving the hospital, because I was afraid that it would get worse. It happened so quickly. I never felt like that before. I started to cry and couldn't stop.

When we got home, everything did get worse. All of a sudden I couldn't get myself out of bed. I didn't have the energy to get up with you every morning and make your lunch for school. So, your daddy had to do it instead. When you were at school your sister cried a lot, and it made me cry even more.

Everything seemed so much harder than it was before. I wanted to take her outside and to the park like you and I used to, but I just couldn't. It felt like someone had stolen the sun. All of my light was gone, and I couldn't get it back. I tried snuggling with your sister and play dates with my friends and their kids. I didn't understand why all of my friends with babies were smiling and laughing when all I wanted to do was cry and go back to bed. I couldn't even get up to wait for you to get off of the school bus. I just felt like sleeping. Nothing made sense anymore.

One day, your daddy and I were talking, and he said he thought it might be a good idea if I went to see someone about my sadness. So, I searched the internet and found someone who could help. She was a therapist. A therapist is the same as a counselor, and they help people who feel sad or anxious. Your grandma came over to watch your sister so I could go talk to the therapist. I spent a whole hour crying and explaining to her how I felt. I thought I had to be the only mom who had ever

felt like that, because I hadn't heard anyone else ever say that I would feel like that after I had a baby. It was so different from when I had you. The therapist explained that I had postpartum depression. She gave me some information to take home and read. She also gave me some activities to try. I went home and read the information she gave me and even did my own research. I wanted so badly to get better, so I decided that I would try everything that I could.

Very slowly I started to get better after following the instructions from the therapist. It was one thing at a time. It started by getting out of bed and getting dressed. After that, I started to eat a healthy breakfast. Before I knew it I was taking your sister out for a walk in her stroller. The walks got longer as the days went by. I felt like the sun was peeking out frombehind the clouds. I was finally back to getting you off the bus and felt like I had a routine again. I felt better and found happiness in all the things that used to make me feel good. You and I were back to making our imaginary worlds and playing in the park. But, my sadness was not totally gone.

I want to make sure that you know that even though I may not have seemed like the same mommy, I was always there way deep down inside. It took me a while, but I got back to being the mommy who tickled you, blew bubbles, and danced in the kitchen. Sometimes mommy may get depressed, but my love for you has never, and will never, change.

Overcoming postpartum depression made me feel like I could now get through anything. I promise I will always try my best to be the mommy that you need me to be. I will never understand why postpartum depression happened. There may not be a reason, but I got through it. I'm here now, and I will never stop loving you, your sister, and our family.

Vocabulary

Depression: feeling of extreme sadness that causes a person to experience a lot of difficulty doing normal daily tasks

Postpartum Depression: depression that a mother feels after she has a baby

The following are questions for you, the adult reader, to ask the child or children in order to have a guided conversation. Change the pronouns as needed based on if you are the parent reading to your child, counselor reading to a client, student, or small group, or however it would best apply.

1. Tell me, in your own words, the meaning of Postpartum depression?
2. Who were the characters in this story?
3. What was this story about?
4. What was the problem in this story?
5. How did it make boy feel when his mom stopped taking care of him?
6. How was the problem solved?
7. Do you understand that boy and his sister did not do anything wrong?
8. Is there anything that the boy's mom could do to help him if this happens again?
9. Is there anything that the boy could do to help his mom?
10. Do you feel safe with your mom?
11. Do you feel that your mom loves you?
12. Is there anything you miss doing with your mom?

Jaa'Lisa Banks is a Dallas, TX native, currently residing in Minneapolis, MN with her husband and 5 kids. After being diagnosed with Bipolar disorder, she began on a journey of healing and understanding. It is her personal mission to help spread awareness about mental illness, especially while being a mom. This book series is one of a kind, and is designed to help parents navigate their mental illness with their kids in a way that they can understand.

You can keep up with Jaa'Lisa on Instagram at @thebundleofbanks or Facebook at @thebanksfamilyblog. She also blogs occasionally at www.bundleofbanks.com.

CPSIA information can be obtained
at www.ICGtesting.com
Printed in the USA
LVHW072010130121
676360LV00022B/1156